MORAG HOOD

BRENDA IS A SHEEP

TW🦉 HOOTS

These are sheep.

This is also a sheep.

This sheep is called Brenda.

Brenda has a very nice woolly jumper.

Brenda does all the
things that sheep do . . .

. . . because Brenda is a sheep.

The sheep learn lots of new games
from their friend Brenda.

Like catch,

teeth sharpening,

and tag. Brenda loves tag.

But no matter how hard she tries ...

 ... she can never catch anyone.
They always get away.

The sheep think Brenda is probably
the best sheep they have ever met.

She is so very tall, has nice pointy teeth,
and her wool is all knitted and colourful.

All the sheep want to be just like Brenda.

But Brenda
has other things
on her mind.

She is working
hard on her special
mint sauce recipe.

The sheep have never had Brenda's special
mint sauce but she tells them it is very tasty.

You just need to find the right thing
to eat it with.

Luckily, Brenda knows just the thing. She is getting ready for a feast.

The sheep are very excited.

Brenda tells the sheep to go to bed nice and early. She says there will be a surprise for them in the morning.

A delicious surprise.

Brenda has to wait a very long
time for the sheep to go to sleep.

But at last they begin to nod off, one by one.
Brenda counts them on her claws.

 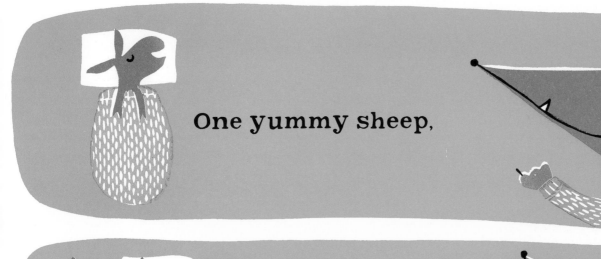

One yummy sheep,

two yummy sheep,

three yummy sheep . . .

ZZZZZZZZZ

BAAAA!

By the time Brenda wakes up, the sheep
have made a surprise of their own.

There is
grass stew

and grass
pie

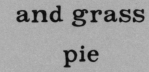

and grass
burgers

and grass
lasagne

and grass
sandwiches

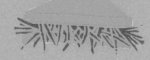

and grass
sausages.

And for pudding,
grass biscuits.

With a delicious
sauce to pour
over it all.

This is not the feast Brenda had planned.

But when she sees everything
her friends have done for her,

BRENDA

BRENDA IS BEST

Brenda can't help but
join in the fun.
Because, after all . . .

Brenda is a sheep.